THE STORY OF LILIANA
A Brave Indigenous Child

Written by **CLARE ROSENFIELD**

Illustrated by **BEATRIZ CORTAZAR**

The Story of Liliana: A Brave Indigenous Girl

Published by Gatekeeper Press
2167 Stringtown Rd, Suite 109
Columbus, OH 43123-2989
www.GatekeeperPress.com

Copyright © 2022 by Clare Rosenfield

All rights reserved. Neither this book, nor any parts within it may be sold or reproduced in any form or by any electronic or mechanical means, including information storage and retrieval systems, without permission in writing from the author. The only exception is by a reviewer, who may quote short excerpts in a review.

ISBN (paperback): 9781662923630

Chapters

CHAPTER ONE	**BEGINNINGS**	1
CHAPTER TWO	**WANDERINGS**	6
CHAPTER THREE	**ALLIES**	10
CHAPTER FOUR	**A NEW FRIEND**	18
CHAPTER FIVE	**THE RETURN OF THE EAGLE**	23
CHAPTER SIX	**HOMECOMING**	28
CHAPTER SEVEN	**RISING ABOVE THE CHALLENGES**	35
CHAPTER EIGHT	**DIVINE REVELATION**	42
ABOUT THE AUTHOR		45

CHAPTER ONE

BEGINNINGS

Once upon a time there was a little girl who had a big wish. She didn't dare tell it to anyone because she was shy and more than that, she didn't belong in the community where she was living. She had been born on a Native American reservation but because during those years, the Caucasian people who claimed to be the owners of her family's land and basically of all the land in the New World which they called America did not want indigenous people to spread their culture and maintain their customs or language, she was no longer living in her indigenous world. It was a painful experience for many children.

And for this little girl, whose name was Liliana, who had been dragged from her parents' arms at the age of two, life had only become bearable by remaining silent most of the time. She was taught to do what her older siblings and what her new Mom and Dad told her to do. If she disobeyed, she would be denied her supper or worse, spanked.

Now she was already nine years old and a very good student at the local school. Her greatest talent was rhyming. She loved to write poems and give them to people on their birthdays. That was the main reason her family was kind to her. Otherwise, she had to wash the dishes, sweep the floors, make everyone's bed, and help make the meals. In other words, the family treated her like a hired servant.

To survive, Liliana began to communicate with everything that was not human. When she was walking to school, she took time to call out to the trees along her unpaved path, silently of course, because she could not let the other children know what she was doing. There was one special tree she became friends with and that was one she leaned up against every day on her way home from school. Coming home she could walk more slowly and take more time in the woods because she did not have to be on time for school. Still, she was expected at home for her chores.

One day, after communing with her special tree, she disappeared. She was nowhere to be found. Her family wondered why she had not come home from school. Did someone kidnap her? Did she run away? They searched the woods, sent dogs and men out to search for her. Where could she have gone?

That is when they began to realize how much they depended on her. The other children were lazy and rarely helped with the chores. Now they would have to pitch in. That is when they realized how hard they had been on her and began to worry she might have ended her life.

CHAPTER TWO

WANDERINGS

Iliana was nowhere to be found. But because of her Native roots and her big wish to find her true family and tribe, she had asked one tree after another in her favorite woods how to find them. The trees guided her telepathically for many miles, through many woods and dales, until she glimpsed in the far distance a lot of smoke. She had heard that her tribe liked to do fire ceremonies and so she made her way over to that smoky territory.

She had not eaten in days but had found shelter at night at the base of a tree in a new forest on her way. That morning luckily she spied some blueberry bushes and picked enough to fill her tummy. During the night, though, she received some special dream messages.

An angelic being came to her telling her, "You are a divine child and you have a special purpose there on your earth."

Liliana murmured in her sleep, "Is it my big wish?"

The angel answered, "It is bigger than your big wish! First, you wish to find your original family, right?"

"Oh yes!"

"Well, I have good news for you. They are looking for you as well and have been doing many sacred ceremonies to call you to them. You are getting close to where they are. And now I will bless you and open your third eye so that you can see them even before you meet them. That way you will recognize them and they will recognize you."

"Oh thank you, my guardian angel! Thank you!"

As the angel blessed her and opened her intuitive third eye, Liliana felt a huge surge of renewed energy to bring forth her life's purpose and fulfill her big wish that even she did not know how to verbalize fully, not yet.

CHAPTER THREE

ALLIES

LILIANA AWAKENED WITH a huge smile on her face and a big warm feeling in her heart. She realized she had been visited by a beautiful dream and tried to remember who and what had come to her. It simply felt as if a great Being had blessed her and opened all the closed doors inside her, giving her hope and optimism and renewed energy for her wanderings.

She picked some more blueberries, walked toward the sound of water falling, and to her surprise, discovered a stream of clean and clear water pouring down from a waterfall on a mountainous ridge and so she dared to slake her thirst. She also washed her face and hands and parts of her body as best she could.

A squirrel came by searching for nuts and recognizing Liliana's hunger, he found a way to beckon her toward a stash of nuts which he invited her to share with him. Liliana was both amazed and grateful that a squirrel could be so lovingly sensitive to her. She realized that her intuition that all the creatures are conscious and able to communicate has been correct all along. Not only are trees her friends, but now all the animals she meets will become friends with whom she can share her concerns, thoughts, and needs.

A fluttering of wings and some loud caws sounded above her from the top of one of the trees. She stopped and asked, "Who are you? Do you have a message for me?"

An eagle responded, "I am one of your guardians and I can take you to your tribe if you are not afraid to ride on my back."

"Oh," Liliana responded. "How can I be sure that you won't take me away to be eaten or what if I fall off?" All her doubts came to the fore. And the eagle flew away, telling her she would be back if Liliana called out to her in her heart of hearts, but she did not want her to be scared.

Liliana felt relieved, but a bit regretful at the same time. She did not know which direction was the right one when a family of deer came by. "Follow us," they suggested.

She felt safe with them and decided to follow. They led her through many forests and open meadows. She still kept the vision of that fire ceremony she felt calling to her through the smoke she had seen in the distance. Had that been her imagination? Perhaps, but she still felt it was calling to her, tugging at her heart, even invisibly.

The deer led her to a vegetable garden where they lingered eating greens and carrots. She was so famished that she too followed their lead, though a part of her worried that she was taking something that did not belong to her.

By the time it was nighttime, when she lay down on the grass to sleep, her guardian angel told her, "Rest easy, my child, sometimes we need to take something that belongs to another family, but truly all of nature belongs to us all, and some day, when you return to this area, you will offer this family and their garden great riches and healing messages."

CHAPTER FOUR

A NEW FRIEND

In the morning, she was awakened by a tap on her shoulder. A little being, neither a human nor an animal, appeared to befriend her. "Who are you?" she asked with genuine curiosity and interest.

"Some call me an elf," he answered. "I don't know what I am but I know what I'm made of."

"What's that?" she asked.

"Stardust and love, greenery and smiles, and a big dose of magic!"

"Wow," she exclaimed. "Can you help me with your magic and all that you are?"

"What do you need?" he asked.

"I am seeking my original family. When I was two years old, I was taken away from them and now that the family I've been with for seven years is mostly mean to me, I decided to journey away from them and toward my real family, where I truly belong."

"I will be happy to help you," he said, with a perky smile on his little face and a glow emanating from his little body.

"How?" she asked.

"Are you good at closing your eyes and imagining, and while imagining, making things come true?"

"I think I could be," she told him.

"All right," he instructed. "Sit here with your back against this beautiful friendly tree. Close your eyes and ask the tree for permission to take this journey to your highest purpose and calling which will be shown to you at the top of the inner universe."

Liliana asked the tree and felt her permission.

Little elf continued, "Glide yourself up your spinal column and up above the Milky Way to a total of seventy rungs to the body of the inner Universe, the Divine which abides in and as your Highest Self."

She was able to glide up to where he directed her.

"Now see that you are no longer just a little girl. You are also an expanded Being with three hundred sixty degree awareness and sight. You are in a realm of Pure Light and Love and you can ask to see way into the distance and into the future here and now. That way you will be imprinted with the exact directions of how to find your family when you descend back into your life as a little girl and keep walking on."

Liliana reveled in this state of luminosity and in the process of asking for directions to find her true family, she was given the message of where her birth family was located, but at the same time, she was told that her true family was everywhere and everyone who exuded genuine love and kindness. Then, she would never again feel that she did not belong; she would belong in her own loving heart and in the company of the humans and creatures and plants and universal elementals who were suffused with love and kindness always all ways.

"Oh, thank you, my dear new friend," Liliana exclaimed to the elf. "I feel my path has become clear and my energy renewed. I am no longer in doubt or afraid."

"Wonderful!" he responded. "Now you can thank the messengers and the Divine Presence you have encountered and follow your inner guidance until you have come to the place you have been seeking all your life. And thank your inner tree for taking you to that height as well."

Liliana did what he told her to do and when she was back, she opened her eyes to see the elf smiling at her and glowing with the same luminosity she sensed in her meditative state. She smiled at him and was overjoyed to feel that she too was glowing back to him.

She exclaimed, "Now I am ready to move forward on this journey. Will you come with me or shall I continue on alone?"

Little elf told her, "Yes, you are ready. I have faith you will find your family all on your own. Eagle will help you. You will see. She will come back, of that I am sure and I will be here for you if you ever return to this woods. And now I shower you with blessings and love! "

Liliana thanked him and said she would look for him again some day.

CHAPTER FIVE

THE RETURN OF THE EAGLE

NOW THAT LILIANA had had such an expansive experience of the height of her inner Universe, she felt unafraid and ready to accept a ride on the eagle's back if she returned. No sooner had she had that thought than she was back.

"I heard your heart and I came back," she said, "to offer my help once more. Would you feel ready to take a ride on my wingspan? I promise not to let you fall off!"

"Gladly," Liliana answered. "Thank you so much for your patience and your understanding."

"No problem!" she said. "Now climb on and bid your little helper friend good-bye. He needs to stay here in this lovely forest."

"Good-bye, dear friend who took me so far and wide in my innermost self! I will never forget you! I hope we will meet again!"

"Yes, Liliana, it was my joy to help you, and have a beautiful journey and a magnificent homecoming with the beloved family who cares so deeply for you and cannot wait to welcome you back."

Now Liliana climbed upon the eagle's back and rested her head on the base of her neck while her arms wrapped gently around her neck and her legs stretched out upon her wingspan, hugging it close.

They flew in a very steady path without many twists and turns so she felt safe and unthreatened. She gazed down and caught sight of a series of smoke signals. "There!" she exclaimed. "That is where I need to land. I believe my family is waiting for me there!"

Eagle lowered them down very gently, very gradually, until they were at the edge of the forest and the clearing from which the smoke was wafting.

Eagle said she would wait for her to make sure that this was the right place.

Lil ana walked slowly, almost holding her breath from excitement, and entered the forest.

CHAPTER SIX

HOMECOMING

A GROUP OF ELDERS observed this little girl walking slowly towards them. They called all the people to come out from their tents and workplaces.

"Come and see who has come home!" they cried.

And many of them ran toward Liliana, pulling her into their arms. She was overwhelmed and started to cry with joy, recognizing that they didn't even need more than a second to recognize her! They knew her. They welcomed her. They were her true family. She had found them. She was so happy. Her journey had been over many weeks but she had arrived. At last she had arrived.

Her birth mother, Lakotiana, came to identify herself to Liliana. "You have come home, my dear angelic child. I have prayed and prayed for your return. Seven long years you have been gone, but not one day has gone by that I have not thought about you. Please know that at last you are home. No one will ever take you away from us again."

Liliana could not speak for how full her heart was; all she could do was cry and hug, hug and cry. Her tears for all the missing years, and her tears for the wondrous miracle of this present homecoming. She told her mother, "The smoke led me to you! I glimpsed it and never forgot it and the eagle helped me to find it and you!" Then she remembered,

"Oh, my eagle is waiting out there to make sure I'm in the right place. Can we go and thank her and let her know she gave us all a great gift?"

"Oh yes, dear child," her Mom and the elders exclaimed. "Let us honor this blessed eagle in our ceremony of thanks that we will do now that you have returned."

And so they found the eagle patiently waiting for the good news and she was invited into the circle, sitting on a branch of a special tree in their midst, and a ceremony was prepared.

"But first, my child, you must be so hungry."

"Yes, I have not eaten a real meal in many weeks."

"How did you survive?"

"Berries and nuts a squirrel friend shared with me and water from streams and a waterfall, and some greens and vegetables in a little garden a deer friend led me to."

"Well, here, my child, sit and eat of our beans and rice, our vegetables and breads, and fill your body once again, as best you can."

Lil ana was able to eat enough to satisfy her little body.

Then the ceremony began. There was dancing and drumming, singing and chanting, praising and praying, thanking and blessing. Everyone participated. Liliana felt like a goddess. She was placed at the center of the ceremony and everyone surrounded her with their love and blessings, as well as eagle to whom they sent love and blessings as well. Liliana remembered the deer and the squirrel who had helped her find food and asked that they be included, and so they were.

CHAPTER SEVEN

RISING ABOVE THE CHALLENGES

After the ceremony and after Liliana's family settled her in to where she would sleep and live her life, the elders conferred. "Shall we tell her?" they asked. What did they mean by that?

There were threats to their way of life. There were pipelines being dug into their ancestors' sacred burial grounds. There were their sources of drinking water being polluted by the chemicals from these pipelines. There were militias standing guard against any of them who stood up for their rights in peaceful protest.

Only a few miles away, there were hundreds of protesters remaining in non-violent stance against the pipeline, but despite their peaceful presence, the militia was using water cannons on them, teargas, rubber bullets, dogs sent to bite them, and water sprayed on them from low-flying helicopters. It was an ongoing threat which carried the history of exploitation and domination from colonial days to this day. It seemed nothing had changed. The banks bankrolling the pipelines and the people profiting from them seemed to hold the power, making it nearly impossible to change things on the ground or change hearts and minds.

Yet that is where they needed to go—to the way of transformation of hearts and minds.

For that, they did ceremonies every day. For that, they called on Mother Earth to support their efforts to protect Her. For that, they founded a non-profit organization to be dedicated to buying back land that was rightfully theirs but which had been confiscated by former colonialists and present-day governments who had no regard for the indigenous peoples of the world.

The elders decided, along with Liliana's mother and father that they were not going to hide these facts from her. Maybe she would be of help. In fact, they felt that she might have a unique approach to all this and so after a good long night's sleep, in the morning, they greeted her and asked her to sit with them.

"Liliana," they said, "We know you are only a nine year old girl, but we want you to help us with a serious threat to our indigenous existence."

Liliana responded, "How could I not know that there are threats? That is what led to my being taken away from you, so I bet some of that is still going on."

"Yes," they continued, "but it is more than our loved ones being taken from us. It is our sacred lands, our way of life, our languages, our burial grounds, our rights as human beings."

"How are they doing that?" she asked.

That is when they told her about the pipelines and the protests and the futility of their attempts to convince the government to ban such ways to exploit the Mother Earth and desecrate their sacred lands.

"What to do?" they asked her. "We think you might have some ideas."

"Yes," she said. "When I was in a particular forest, a little elf came to help me. He guided me to my inner Universe which was my own Higher Self I could rise up from within my spine, up to seventy levels way above the Milky Way, and there I would find luminosity and three hundred sixty degree vision and power to fulfill my deepest wishes and intentions which I have carried with me all my life. That wish was to find you, my family."

They all sighed in recognition of this wise child's words.

"And," she added, "I was told that you are not my only family, that within me and within us all, there is a true inner family, a true inner Divinity that never leaves us and always guides us and aligns us with our highest good. And that is how I now know that whatever happens, wherever I am, I am at home, at home inside my own Higher Self."

The elders were very uplifted and said, "And so let us each enter into that Divine Presence. Let us follow our child's guidance."

Liliana then shared what she had learned from the elf, "Close your eyes and find your innermost tree, your Tree of Life. Ask its permission to rise to the height of yourselves and do healing and intention-setting. Pretend your spinal column is a ladder or an elevator and rise up to the seventieth level where you can sit and bask in the luminous Presence of the Divine and ask for what is in the highest good for all beings in the universe."

And so each one spoke aloud what each perceived to be in the highest good for all,

"May all beings be free to live, evolve, and blossom!"

"May no one be a victim of harmful thoughts or actions. May all feel welcome in this world."

"May we create peace from our peaceful hearts and envision peace in our world here and now!"

"May we harbor no resentment and forgive all now."

"May the Divine transform all minds, open all hearts, and align all with global harmony and global justice!"

"May all negative influences inner and outer be removed from this world and from all minds and hearts."

"May we always be in close touch with our innermost knowing, our Divine guidance."

"May we live as a blessing to everyone we meet as well as to ourselves and our closest ones."

"May we be a soothing, healing presence in the world."

CHAPTER EIGHT
DIVINE REVELATION

AFTER THE PRAYERS came to a close, an Oracle among them rose to speak.

"I have received a message from on high."

"Speak," they encouraged him. "We are all ears."

"We are a microcosm of the macrocosm. Our struggle for our continued existence and for our rights is a mirror of what our Mother Earth is experiencing as a result of humans disrespecting Her right to an intact body and as a result of ignorance. We are the ones to awaken the world to the truth. We are not the only ones but we knew from eons ago that if the icecaps begin to melt, it spells disaster for our beloved home, our planet."

"We are the ones who respect women and the Feminine, another group like Mother Earth who is being held back and hurt. We are the ones who can communicate with the creatures and the forests and the plants and who want to save them before they go extinct, because when and if they do, humans will eventually go extinct as well.

"Therefore, we have a powerful responsibility to inform the world of how to reverse the damage and how to give back to Mother Earth instead of taking more, robbing Her of her minerals and layers of soil and rock and mountaintops and polluting her circulatory system, her waterways. We can and must go to speak first to those who will be open to hearing us and becoming our allies, and then en masse, go to the ones perpetuating the denials and the damage and change their hearts and their ways."

"Yes, yes, yes," they all murmured. "May the work begin!"

And Liliana felt she had come to the right place at the right time and even though she was just a small child, she would be able to join her family and the tribe and the elders and make her best contribution.

ABOUT THE AUTHOR

CLARE ROSENFIELD

After receiving both an M.A. in French and teaching French, and an M.S. in Social Work, and practicing as a Licensed Clinical Social Worker, Clare Rosenfield became moved by the plight of the Earth and of all those whose voices and rights have been suppressed, in particular, indigenous peoples worldwide.

Her self-illustrated poetry collection of 29 poems and 17 illustrations, ROLL ON GREAT EARTH, which she published in 2002, was her call to jolt people from their lack of compassion, sense of despair or unquestioned acceptance of war into the realization that there is a chance for peace and it is within each one's reach. Her poems offer a glimpse of how to connect from your heart to all beings, including animals, plants, the living earth, and all life.

Her verse narrative THE CALL OF MOTHER EARTH: How a Being of Light Draws Forth Humanity's Response which she printed in 2004, 2017, and again in 2021, is to awaken human beings to the plight of our Earthmother and how to help heal Her by expressing their love and appreciation for Her from the depths of everyone's hearts.

As President of the Global Healing Foundation (www.globalhealingfoundation.org) Clare has become acutely aware of the way indigenous peoples, cultures, and sacred lands have been abused and their rights trampled worldwide. This inspired The Story of Liliana which features a little girl who had been forcibly removed from her original indigenous family home and placed in a home where she felt mistreated. Her courage to walk away leads to wondrous results.

In addition to eight poetry collections and essays printed in various journals, Clare has written other children's stories, including Seven Meditations for Children, SUN-CHILD, The Sleeping Giantess Wakes Up, The Little Girl Who Wanted to be a Tree, and others. Her earlier publications include a co-authored book on Siamese temple paintings and Jataka tales written during her six years in Thailand, booklets on reverence for all life, vegetarianism, and universal prayers for peace, a biography of her Jain guru, and books she edited of his talks. She has been a teacher of various forms of meditation for over fifty years, and plays the harp for meditation circles and end-of-life care.

Her son and daughter and their families have given her the joy of six grandchildren, all of whom are artistic, musical, and caring human beings.

Beatriz Cortazar, the illustrator, is her friend, originally from Colombia, South America, which makes this story even more relevant when we pray that the sacred lands of the indigenous in Colombia be protected and their rights respected.

www.ingramcontent.com/pod-product-compliance
Lightning Source LLC
LaVergne TN
LVHW072019060526
838200LV00062B/4901